DATE DUE

DEC 0 2 2013			

FORTUNATELY,
THE MILK

OTHER BOOKS BY
NEIL GAIMAN

Blueberry Girl

Chu's Day

Coraline

Crazy Hair

The Dangerous Alphabet

The Day I Swapped My Dad for Two Goldfish

The Graveyard Book

Instructions

InterWorld

MirrorMask

M Is for Magic

Odd and the Frost Giants

Stardust

The Wolves in the Walls

FORTUNATELY, THE MILK

BY NEIL GAIMAN

ILLUSTRATED BY SKOTTIE YOUNG

HARPER

An Imprint of HarperCollins*Publishers*

Fortunately, the Milk
Text copyright © 2013 by Neil Gaiman
Illustrations copyright © 2013 by Skottie Young

Library of Congress Cataloging-in-Publication Data
Gaiman, Neil.
  Fortunately, the milk / by Neil Gaiman ; illustrated by Skottie
Young. — First edition.
     pages cm
  Summary: While picking up milk for his children's cereal, a
father is abducted by aliens and finds himself on a wild adventure
through time and space.
  ISBN 978-0-06-222407-1 (hardcover bdgs)
  ISBN 978-0-06-229515-6 (int'l ed.)
  [1. Adventure and adventurers—Fiction. 2. Space and time—
Fiction. 3. Fathers—Fiction. 4. Humorous stories.] I. Young,
Skottie, illustrator. II. Title.
PZ7.G1273Fo 2013   2012050670
[Fic]—dc23   CIP
                                                          AC

Typography by Sarah Nichole Kaufman
13 14 15 16 17   LP/RRDH   10 9 8 7 6 5 4 3 2 1
❖
First Edition

There was only orange juice in the fridge. Nothing else that you could put on cereal, unless you think that ketchup or mayonnaise or pickle juice would be nice on your Toastios, which I do not, and neither did my little sister, although she has eaten some pretty weird things in her day, like mushrooms in chocolate.*

"No milk," said my sister.

"Nope," I said, looking behind the jam in the fridge, just in case. "None at all."

*She did not actually like eating them. And I had not actually told her that there were mushrooms inside the chocolate. It was an experiment.

Our mum had gone off to a conference. She was presenting a paper on lizards. Before she went, she reminded us of the important things that had to happen while she was away.

My dad was reading the paper. I do not think he pays a lot of attention to the world while he is reading his paper.

"Did you hear me?" asked my mum, who is suspicious. "What did I say?"

"Do not forget to take the kids to Orchestra Practice on Saturday; it's Violin on Wednesday night; you've frozen a dinner for each night you're away and labeled them; the spare house-key is with the Nicolsons; the plumber will be here on Monday morning and do not use or flush the upstairs toilet until he's been; feed the goldfish; you love us and you'll be back on Thursday," said my father.

I think my mum was surprised. "Yes, that's right," she said. She kissed us all. Then she said, "Oh, and we're almost out of milk. You'll need to pick some up."

After she went away, my dad had a cup of tea. There was still some milk left.

We defrosted Meal Number One, but we made a bit of a mess of things, so we went to the Indian restaurant. Before we went to sleep, Dad made us mugs of hot chocolate to make up for the whole **MissinG of Mum.**

THAT WAS
last
night.

Now Dad came in. "Eat your cereal," he said. "Remember, it's Orchestra Practice this afternoon."

"We can't eat our cereal," said my sister, sadly.

"I don't see why not," said my father. "We've got plenty of cereal. There's Toastios and there's muesli. We have bowls. We have spoons. Spoons are excellent. Sort of like forks, only not as stabby."

"No milk," I said.

"No milk," said my sister.

I watched my dad think about this. He looked like he was going to suggest that we have something for breakfast that you do not need milk for, like sausages, but then he looked like he remembered that, without milk, he couldn't have his tea. He had his "no tea" face.

"You poor children," he said. "I will walk down to the shop on the corner. I will get milk."

"Thank you," said my sister.

"Not the fat-free kind," I told him. "That stuff tastes like water."

"Right," said my dad. "Not the fat-free kind."

He went out.

I poured some Toastios into a bowl. I stared at them.

I waited.

"How long has he been?" asked my sister.

"Ages," I said.

"I thought so," said my little sister.

We drank orange juice. My sister practiced her violin. I suggested that she stop playing her violin, and she did.

My sister made faces at me.

"How long has it been now?" she asked.

"Ages and ages," I told her.

"What happens if he never comes back?" she asked.

"I suppose we eat the pickles," I said.

"You can't eat pickles for breakfast," said my sister. "And I don't like pickles at any time. What if something awful has happened to him? Mum would blame us."

"I expect he just ran into one of his friends at the corner shop," I said, "and they got talking and he lost track of time."

I ate a dry Toastio as an experiment. It was sort of okay, but not as good as in milk.

There was a thump and a bang at the front door, and my father came in.

"Where have you been all this time?" asked my sister.

"Ah," said my father. "Um. Yes. Well, funny you should ask me that."

"You ran into someone you knew," I said, "and you lost track of time."

"I bought the milk," said my father. "And I did indeed say a brief hello to Mister Ronson from over the road, who was buying a paper. I walked out of the corner shop, and heard something odd that seemed to be coming from above me. It was a noise like this: *thummthumm*. I looked up and saw a huge silver disc hovering in the air above Marshall Road."

"*Hullo*," I said to myself. "*That's not something you see every day.* And then something odd happened."

"*That* wasn't odd?" I asked.

"Well, something **ODDER**," said my father. "The odd thing was the beam of light that came out of the disc—a glittery, shimmery beam of light that was visible even in the daylight. And the next thing I knew, I was being sucked up into the disc. **Fortunately, I had put the milk into my coat pocket.**

"The deck of the disc was metal. It was as big as a playing field, or B I G G E R."

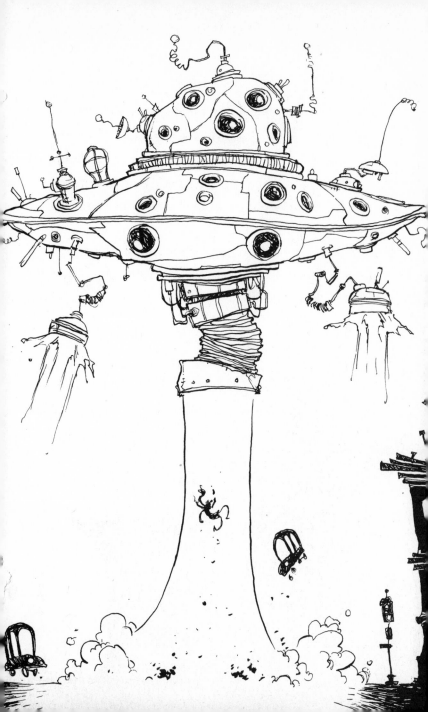

"We have come to your planet from a world very far away," said the people in the disc.

I call them people, but they were a bit green and rather globby and they looked very grumpy indeed.

"Now, as a representative of your species, we demand that you give us ownership of the whole planet. We are going to remodel it."

"I jolly well won't," I said.

"Then," it said, "we will bring all your enemies here and have them make you miserable until you agree to sign the planet over to us."

I was going to point out to them that I didn't have any enemies when I noticed a large metal door with

EMERGENCY EXIT
DO NOT OPEN FOR ANY REASON
THIS MEANS YOU!

on it. I opened the door.

"Don't do that," said a green, globby person. "You'll let the space-time continuum in."

But it was too late; I had already pushed open the door.

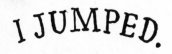

I JUMPED.

I was

FALLING.

Fortunately, I had kept tight hold of the milk, so when I splashed into the sea I didn't lose it.

"What was that?" said a woman's voice. "A big fish? A mermaid? Or was it a spy?"

I wanted to say that I wasn't any of those things, but my mouth was full of seawater. I felt myself being hauled up onto the deck of a little ship. There were a number of men and a woman on the deck, and they all looked very cross.

"Who be ye, landlubber?" said the woman, who had a big hat on her head and a parrot on her shoulder.

"He's a spy! A walrus in a coat! A new kind of mermaid with legs!" said the men.

"What are you doing here?" asked the woman.

"Well," I said. "I just set out to the corner shop for some milk for my children's breakfast and for my tea, and the next thing I knew—"

"He's lying, Your Majesty!"

She pulled out her cutlass. "You dare lie to the Queen of the Pirates?"

Fortunately, I had kept tight hold of the milk, **and now I pointed to it**.

"If I did not go to the corner shop to fetch the milk," I asked them, "then *where* did this milk come from?"

At this, the pirates were completely speechless. "Now," I said, "if you could let me off somewhere near to my destination, I would be much obliged to you."

"And where would that happen to be?" said
the Queen of the Pirates.

"On the corner of Marshall Road and Fletcher Lane," I said. "My children are waiting there for their breakfast."

"You're on a pirate ship now, my fine bucko," said the Pirate Queen. "And you don't get dropped off anywhere. There are only two choices—you can join my pirate crew, or refuse to join and we will slit your cowardly throat and you will go to the bottom of the sea, where you will feed the fishes."

"What about walking the plank?" I asked.

"NEVER heard of it!" said the pirates.

"Walking the plank!" I said. "It's what proper pirates do! Look, I'll show you. Do you have a plank anywhere?"

It took some looking, but we found a plank, and I showed the pirates where to put it. We discussed nailing it down, but the Pirate Queen decided it was safer just to have the two fattest pirates sit on the end of it.

"Why exactly do you want to walk the plank?" asked the Pirate Queen.

I edged out onto the plank. The blue Caribbean water splashed gently beneath me.

"Well," I said, "I've seen lots of stories with pirates in them, and it seems to me that if I'm going to be rescued—"

At this, the pirates started to laugh so hard their stomachs wobbled, and the parrot took off into the air in amazement. "Rescue?" they said. "There's no rescue out here. We're in the middle of the sea."

"Nevertheless," I told them. "If you are going to be rescued, it will always be while walking the plank."

"Which we don't do," said the Pirate Queen. "Here. Have a **SPANISH DOUBLOON** and come and join us in our piratical adventures. It's the eighteenth century," she added, "and there's always room for a bright, enthusiastic pirate."

I caught the doubloon. "I almost wish that I could," I told her. "But I have children. And they need their breakfast."

"Then you must die! Walk the plank!"

I edged out to the end of the plank. Sharks were circling. So were piranhas—

And this was where

I interrupted my dad for

THE FIRST TIME.

"Hang on," I said. "Piranhas are a freshwater fish. What were they doing in the sea?"

"You're right," said my father. "The
piranhas were later. Right. So . . ."

I was out at the end of the plank, facing certain death, when a rope ladder hit my shoulder and a deep, booming voice shouted,

I needed no more encouragement than this, and I grabbed the rope ladder with both hands. **Fortunately, the milk was pushed deep into the pocket of my coat.** The pirates hurled insults at me, and even discharged pistols, but neither insults nor pistol-shot found their targets and I soon made it to the top of the rope ladder.

I'd never been in the basket of a hot air balloon before. It was very peaceful up there.

The person in the balloon basket said, "I hope you don't mind me helping, but it looked like you were having problems down there."

I said, "You're a stegosaurus!"

"I am an inventor," he said. "I have invented the

thing we are traveling in, which I call Professor Steg's Floaty-Ball-Person-Carrier."

"I call it a balloon," I said.

"Professor Steg's Floaty-Ball-Person-Carrier is the original name," he said. "And right now we are one hundred and fifty million years in the future."

"Actually," I said, "we are about three hundred years in the past."

"Do you like hard-hairy-wet-white-crunchers?" he asked.

"Coconuts?" I guessed.

"I named them first," said Professor Steg. He picked up a coconut from a basket and ate it, shell and all, just as you or I might crunch toast.

He showed me his Time Machine. He was very proud of it. It was a large cardboard box with several pebbles on it, and stones stuck to the side. There was also a large, red button. I looked at the stones. "Hang on," I said. "Those are diamonds. And sapphires. And rubies."

"Actually," he said, "I call them special-shiny-clear-stones, special-shiny-bluey-stones, and, um—"

"Special-shiny-red-stones?" I suggested.

"Indeed," he said. "I called them that when I was inventing my Really Good Moves Around in Time Machine, one hundred and fifty million years ago."

"Well," I told him, "it was very lucky for me that you turned up when you did and rescued me. I am slightly lost in space and time right now and need to get home in order to make sure my children get milk for their breakfast." I showed it to him. "**This is the milk**. Although I expect that one hundred and fifty million years ago you called it 'wet-white-drinky-stuff.'"

"Dinosaurs are reptiles, sir," said Professor Steg. "We do not go in for milk."

"Do you go in for breakfast cereal?" I asked.

"Of course!" he said. "Dinosaurs **LOVE**

breakfast cereal. Especially the kind with nuts in."

"What do you have on your cereal?" I asked.

"Orange juice, mostly. Or we just eat it dry. But I shall put this in my book: In the distant future, small mammals put milk on their breakfast cereal. I shall write a wonderful book, when I return to the present."

"Actually," I said, "I think this is definitely the past. It has pirates in it."

"It's the future," he said.

"All the dinosaurs have gone off into the stars, leaving the world to mammals."

"I wondered where you all went," I said.

"The stars," he told me. "That is where we will have gone."

"So," I said. "Can you take me home?"

"Well," he said. "Yes and no."

"What does that mean?"

"Yes, I would love to take you home. Nothing would make me happier. No, I cannot take you home. In all honesty, I do not believe that I can take **me** home. My Time Machine is being temperamental. I need a special-shiny-greeny-stone. I have pressed that button many times but nothing happens."

"*Button?* Don't you mean 'big-red-flat-pressy-thing'?" I asked.

"I most certainly do not. It is a button. I named it after my Aunt Button."

"Can I press it?"

"If you wish."

I pressed the button. The sun shot around

the sky, and the sky started to flicker in nights and in days, and the balloon began to rock and lurch and zoom around like an angry fly.

I held on to the ropes as hard as I could. **Fortunately, I was still keeping tight hold of the milk in my right hand.**

When we stopped being blown all across the sky, it was night and, according to Professor Steg, we had only gone back about a thousand years. The moon was nearly full.

"I am even further from my children and our breakfast," I said.

"You have your milk," he said. "Where there is milk, there is hope. Ah, over there. That looks like a perfect landing platform for time-traveling scientists in Floaty-Ball-Person-Carriers."

We landed on the platform and got out. The platform stuck up out of the jungle and had flaming torches on each side. There were people standing on it with very black hair and sharp stone knives.

"Is this a balloon-landing platform?" I asked the people.

"It is not," said a fat man. "It is our temple. We had a very bad harvest last year and we had just asked the gods to send us a sacrifice, to make sure that this year's harvest is better, when you floated down in that thing, with your monster."

"Thank you, by the way," said a little thin man. "I was going to be the sacrifice if no one else turned up. Much obliged."

"So now we will sacrifice you and your monster."

"But my children are waiting for their breakfast," I said. "Look!" I held up the milk.

"Why did they all just fall to their knees?" asked Professor Steg. "Is this usual hairless mammal behavior? Perhaps I should hold up some hard-hairy-wet-white-crunchers and see what happens."

"Coconuts!" I told him. "They are called coconuts!"

"What is that you are holding?" the fat man asked.

"Milk," I said.

"MILK!" they exclaimed, and they prostrated themselves on the ground.

"We have a prophecy," said the fat man, "that when a man and a spiny-backed monster descend from the skies on a round floaty thing—"

"Floaty-Ball-Person-Carrier," said the little thin man.

"Yes. One of those. We were told that when that happened, if the man held up milk then we were not to sacrifice them, but we were meant to take them to the volcano, and give them, as a present, the green jewel that is the Eye of Splod."

"Splod?"

"He is the god of people with short, funny names."

"It is," I said, "a remarkably specific sort of a prophecy. When did you receive it?"

"Last Wednesday," said the fat man, proudly. "The priest of Splod was woken in the night by a

voice whispering from the heavens. And when he went to look and see who it was, there was nobody there. Also, he was sleeping on the top of the temple, and nobody else could have been

up there with him. So it must have either been Splod himself talking, or one of his angelic messengers."

We walked together down a jungle path. Professor Steg carried the rope in his mouth that led up to the balloon, and he dragged the balloon along. After half an hour we reached the volcano.

It was not a very big volcano. There were wisps of smoke coming from the top of it.

On the side of the volcano there was a carving of a big scary face with one eye in the middle of its forehead. The eye was the biggest emerald I had ever seen.

"A special-shiny-greeny-stone!" said Professor Steg, with his mouth full of rope.

The fat man clambered up the side of the volcano.

"It is a good thing that Splod himself told us to give you the Eye of Splod," said the little thin man who had narrowly avoided being sacrificed, "because there is another prophecy that if the Eye of Splod is ever removed, Great Splod will awaken and spread burning destruction across the land."

"Here you go," said the fat man.

He handed us the emerald. Professor Steg nipped up the rope ladder into the balloon's gondola and began to install the emerald in the Time Machine.

"Hang on. He was a stegosaurus?"

"Yes."

"Then how could he just nip up a rope ladder?"

"HE WAS," SAID MY FATHER, "A LARGE STEGOSAURUS, BUT VERY LIGHT ON HIS FEET. THERE ARE FAT PEOPLE WHO ARE EXCELLENT DANCERS."

"Are there any ponies in this?" asked my sister. "I thought there would be ponies by now."

I was standing on the ground, holding on to the rope ladder, when the ground shook and the very small volcano began to belch smoke and lava.

"Splod is angry!" shouted the little thin man. "He wants his eye back."

There was a rushing wind, and the balloon jerked me up into the air, high above the splurting lava.

Unfortunately, I dropped the milk. I wasn't holding on to it tightly enough. It landed on the top of Splod's head.

Professor Steg hauled the rope ladder up with his tail.

"I'VE LOST THE MILK!" I told him.

"That's not good," he admitted.

"But I know where it is. It's on top of Splod's head, on the side of the volcano."

Professor Steg said, "Good Splod! What on earth is that?"

Before our eyes, another balloon, just like ours, appeared, over by the volcano. A man

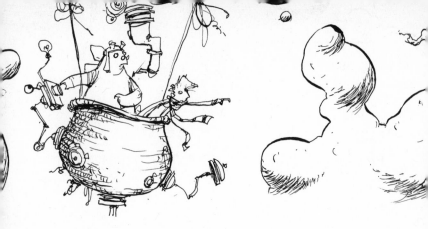

hurried down the rope ladder. He placed a large
emerald in Splod's eye, picked up the milk from
Splod's head, ran up the ladder, and the balloon
vanished.

The very small volcano stopped erupting as
suddenly as if it had been turned off.

"That was a bit peculiar, wasn't it?" said the
professor.

"It was," I agreed, gloom and despair and
despondency overcoming me. "That man in that
balloon stole my milk. We are lost in the past,
with jungles and pirates and volcanoes. Now
I will never get home. My children will never
have breakfast. We are doomed to float forever
through the dusty air of the past in a hot air
balloon."

"It is not a balloon," said Professor Steg. "It is a Floaty-Ball-Person-Carrier. What nonsense you do talk. Now, I think *that* should do the trick."

He finished attaching the emerald to the box, using string, mostly, and also sticky tape, and he pushed the red button.

"Where are we going?" I asked. It seemed like the sun was zooming across the sky, as if nights were following days in a flickering strobe.

"The far, far future!" said Professor Steg.

The machine stopped.

We were hanging in the air above a grassy plain, with a very small grey mountain beneath us.

"There," said Professor Steg. "It is now an extinct volcano. **BUT LOOK!**"

On the side of the extinct volcano was carved the face of Splod, still recognizable, even though it was much eroded by time and the weather, and in the single eye was a huge green emerald, a perfect twin to the one that we had attached to the Time Machine.

"Right," said Professor Steg. "Grab me that special-shiny-greeny-stone."

I went over the side of the gondola and down the rope ladder. I pulled the emerald out of the eye socket.

Below me, on the plain, a number of brightly colored ponies were gathered, and when I picked up the emerald, one of them shouted up at me. "You must be the man without the milk. We have heard about you, in our tales."

"Why are you a pink pony with a pale blue star on the side?" I asked.

"I know," said the pony with a sigh. "It's what everybody's wearing these days. Pale blue stars are *so* last year."

Professor Steg leaned over the side of the balloon's basket. "Hurry up!" he called. "If the volcano is going to go off, it will do it any moment."

The volcano made a noise like a huge burp, and the middle of it collapsed into itself.

"We thought it would do that," said a green pony with a sparkly mane.

"There was a prophecy, I suppose," I said.

"No. We're just very clever." All the ponies nodded. They were very clever ponies.

"I am so glad there were ponies,"
said my sister.

I got back into the balloon basket. Professor Steg unhooked the first emerald from his Time Machine and replaced it with the one that I had just taken from the weathered face of Splod-in-the-Future.

"Do not, whatever else you might do," said the professor, "touch those two stones together."

"Why not?"

"Because, according to my calculations, if the same object from two different times touches itself, one of two things will happen. Either the Universe will cease to exist. Or three remarkable dwarfs will dance through the streets with flowerpots on their heads."

"That sounds astonishingly specific," I said.

"I know. But it is *science*. And it is much more probable that the Universe will end."

"I thought it would be," I said.

"You look so sad," Professor Steg told me.

"I am! It's the milk. My children are breakfastless—"

"The milk!" said Professor Steg. "Of course!" And with that, Professor Steg pressed the red button with his heavily armored tail.

There was a *ZOOM*, a **TWORP**, and a **THANG**, and we were hurtling through the cosmic void.

And then it was dark.

Very dark.

"Oops," said Professor Steg. "Overshot a little. Only by a week, though. Hold on. . . ."

Professor Steg leaned over the side of the basket.

"Excuse me?" he said. "Is there anyone around?"

"Only me," said a very surprised-sounding voice from below us. "The priest of Splod. Who is that up in the sky? Is it a bird? You do not sound like a bird."

"I am not a bird," said Professor Steg. "I am a marvelous yet mysterious and prophetic voice, telling you a mighty prophecy. So mighty that . . . Um . . . Very mighty indeed. Listen. When a huge and good-looking spiny-backed individual—"

"Monster," I told him. "The prophecy said monster."

"Accompanied by a scrawny human being of revolting appearance—" said Professor Steg.

"That was not necessary."

"—lands in a Floaty-Ball-Person-Carrier, you must not sacrifice them. You must instead take them to the volcano and give them the Eye of Splod. And this shall be the way that you shall know them. The human being will hold up some milk."

"Is that the prophecy?" said the voice.

"Yes."

"Is there anything about crops in it?"

"I'm afraid not."

"Oh well. Thank you anyway, prophetic and mysterious voices from the air."

I pressed the red button.

Daylight. We were in the middle of a very familiar volcanic eruption. "Quickly!" I said. "Give me the emerald!"

A little way away I could see a balloon being blown through the sky, while fire and ash were swept around it by the wind. I could see me in the balloon, standing next to Professor Steg, with my mouth open. I looked miserable.

Professor Steg—MY Professor Steg—gave me the emerald.

I raced down the rope ladder and placed the emerald back into the face's eye. Then, as the volcano stopped erupting, I looked around for the milk. I knew it had landed on Splod's head when it fell.

Fortunately, the milk had fallen into a small drift of volcanic ash, and was unharmed. I picked it up, brushed it off, and started back up the balloon ladder. Professor Steg pressed the button.

The sky went dark.

We were *FLOATING* above a landscape of ominous towers and disquieting castles. It was not a friendly place. Bats flew across the sky in huge flocks, crowding out the waning moon.

"I don't like this place," I told the professor.

"I don't see why not," he said. "It looks as if it would be very nice when the sun comes up."

There was a loud FLUT!, and where the bats had been fluttering, several pallid people were now standing. The man in front had a very bald head.

THEY ALL HAD
SHARP TEETH.

"Ve are wumpires," they said. "Vot is this? Who are you? Answer us, or ve vill wiwisect you."

"I am Professor Steg," boomed the Stegosaurus. "This is my assistant. We are on an important mission. I am trying to get back to the present. My assistant is trying to get home to the future for breakfast."

At the word BREAKFAST all the wumpires looked very excited.

"Ve have not had our breakfast," they told us. "Ve normally have vigglyvorms, vith orange juice on them. Orange juice makes vorms ewen vigglier. Like vandering spaghetti. But if ve cannot eat vorms ve vill eat assistant, or ewen roast professor."

One of the wumpires took out a fork, and looked me up and down in a hungry sort of way.

The baldest, most bulging-eyed, rattiest of the wumpires said, "Vot is this box?"

"It is my finest invention," began Professor Steg proudly, but I interrupted.

"It is to keep sandwiches in," I said.

"Sandviches?" said the wumpire.

"Sandwiches," I said, with as much certainty as I could muster.

"Ve thought it vos a Time Machine," said the head wumpire, with a sly, sharp smile. "And ve could use it to inwade the vorld!"

"Definitely sandwiches," I told him.

"Vot happens if I press this button, then?" asked a lady wumpire. She had long black hair that covered most of her face, and peered out at the world with one suspicious eye.

She pressed the button. We went forward six hours in time.

"See?" said the professor happily. "All this place needs to brighten it up is a little bit of sunshine."

The head wumpire said, "Vot?" and dissolved into a cloud of oily black smoke. So did all his friends.

"Yes," I said. "It is a nice place here, after all. In the daylight."

The professor tinkered with the jewels and the string and the buttons. Then he said, "I think I've got it properly fine-tuned, now. This next press should bring you back to your own time, place, and breakfast."

But before the tip of his tail could touch the button, a voice said, "I'll explain later. Fate of the world at stake."

A hand grabbed, and the milk, which I had carried safely for so long, was gone. I turned in time to catch a glimpse of a fine-looking gentleman with his back to me, holding my milk, and then the hole in space through which he had reached was closed.

"MY MILK!"

"He said he'd explain later," said the professor. "I'd be inclined to believe him."

The hole in space opened again. A voice shouted, "Catch!" and the milk came rocketing through.

Fortunately, the milk struck me in the stomach, and in clutching my hands to my belly I caught the milk.

"There," said the professor. "Everything is back to normal."

"He did say he'd explain later," I pointed out. "And that wasn't much of an explanation."

"But it's not later yet," said Professor Steg.

"It's still now. It won't be later until later."

He was arranging pebbles and stones and string on the top of the Time Machine box. "Final coordinates entered," he said. "And then it's off to your house for breakfast."

"Does that mean that there is a Stegosaurus in a hot air balloon outside?" I asked my dad.

"THERE IS NOT," HE SAID. "FOR REASONS THAT WILL BECOME APPARENT."

"I think that there should have been some nice wumpires," said my sister, wistfully. "Nice, handsome, misunderstood wumpires."

"THERE WERE NOT," SAID MY FATHER.

"Would you like to press the button?" said Professor Steg.

I pressed the red button. There was an ear-popping noise and a flicker of years and I was floating, in a balloon basket, above the intersection of Marshall Road and Fletcher Lane. I could see our house from above. I could see the bicycles in the back garden. I could see the rabbit hutch.

"We're here!" I said, and I patted Professor Steg on the back ridge-plates.

"It was very nice, having you as a traveling compani—aargh," said the professor, because there was a familiar sort of a *thumm-thumm* noise, and before I had a chance to press the red button, we were deposited, balloon and all, on the enormous metal deck of a flying saucer, with a number of very grumpy-looking green globby people staring at us with too many eyes. They did not look pleased.

"Ha**HA**!" said several globby people at the same time. "You thought you had escaped us! And you were wrong! Now, you must sign the planet over to us so that we can remodel it. We will take out all the trees, for a start, and put in plastic flamingoes."

"Why?"

"We like plastic flamingoes. We think they are the highest and finest art form that Earth has achieved. And they are tidier than trees."

"Also, we are going to replace the clouds with scented candles."

"We like scented candles, too," explained a huge green globby person, who looked like he was mostly made of snot.

"We also like decorative plates!" said another. "We will put a decorative plate up where the moon is now."

"A really **BiG** decorative plate, showing landmarks of the world."

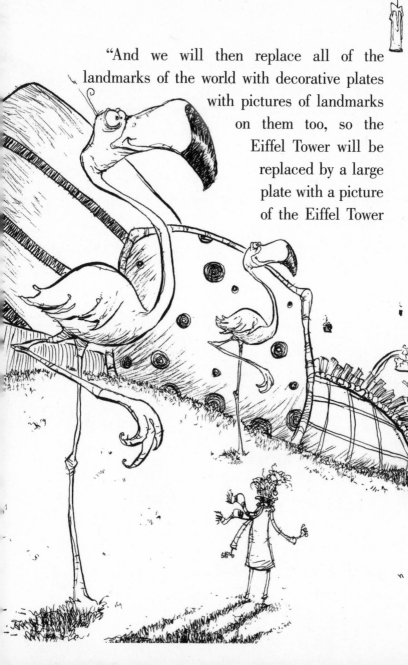

"And we will then replace all of the landmarks of the world with decorative plates with pictures of landmarks on them too, so the Eiffel Tower will be replaced by a large plate with a picture of the Eiffel Tower on it. And Australia will be replaced by a really seriously big plate with Australia on it."

"Also we will replace all of your mountains with throw-cushions," said the smallest, globbiest thing of all, with triumph in its glutinous voice.

"We have learned a lot from our previous meeting," said some globs that were sticking to a wall. "If you look over there, you will see that the door to the space-time continuum you used to escape through last time is now securely locked."

It was definitely locked. It had a huge padlock on it, and a sign saying

KEEP OUT

on it, in unfriendly red letters. There were also chains around it, a tape that said

DO NOT CROSS,

and a handwritten notice that said

For Your Convenience,
Please Use Another Door.

ESCAPE WAS IMPOSSIBLE.

"Also we have depowered your Time Machine."

I looked at the professor. His armored back-flaps were drooping, and his tail was—well, not actually between his legs, because stegosauruses aren't made that way, but if they were, it would have been.

"We have been tracking your movements through time and space," said a large globby alien in front of a console with a screen on it.

"Now, see what happens when I press this **grundledorfer**," said a particularly drippy alien. It was half-sticking to the wall, next to a large black, shiny button.

"It's called a button," I said.

"Nonsense. We named it after our brood-aunt, Nessie Grundledorfer," said the globby aliens. The particularly drippy alien pressed the black button on the metal wall with something that might have been a finger and might just have been a long strand of snot.

There was a CRACKLE.

There was a FIZZ.

Standing around us, in attitudes of anger and irritation, were several pirates, some of the black-haired people from the jungle, a very unhappy-looking volcano god, a large bowl filled with piranhas, and some wumpires.

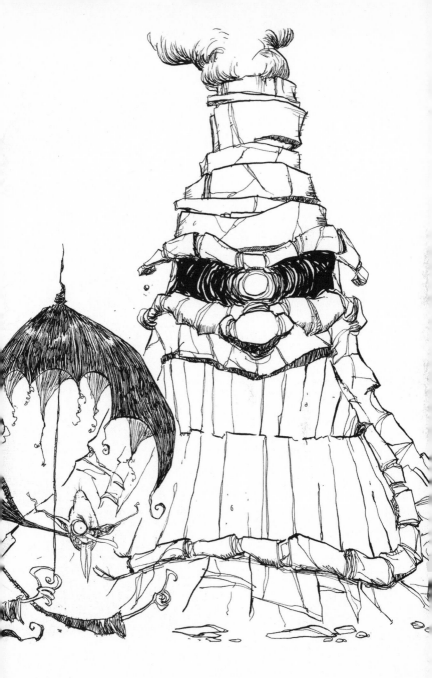

"I'm not sure that I understand what the piranhas are doing," said my sister.

"THEY WERE FROM A NARROW ESCAPE EARLIER THAT I FORGOT TO MENTION," SAID OUR FATHER. "FORTUNATELY, THE MILK FLOATED AT A CRUCIAL MOMENT AND IT ALL ENDED FOR THE BEST."

"I thought it might," I said.

"Uh-oh," I said.

"Prepare to be keelhauled, you scurvy dogs," shouted the pirates.

"Let us now sacrifice them both to great Splod!" shouted the men with shiny black hair.

"They stole my eye! Twice!" rumbled mighty Splod.

"Ve vants those villains and warmints wiolently vound up," proclaimed a tall lady wumpire with long fingernails.

The piranhas said nothing, but they thrashed about in their bowl, ominously.

"Doomed," moaned Professor Steg. "We cannot escape. They have frozen us in time and depowered us. Even my mighty Time Machine can do no more than open a small window in time and space—smaller than either of us could get through."

"But can you do it?" I asked. "Open a little window in time to our last location?"

"Of course. But what good would that do?"

"Quickly!" I said. "Do it!"

Professor Steg pushed the button on the box with the tip of his nose.

There was a ZUM! and a plip! and a window opened in space and time, large enough for an arm to get through.

I reached into it.

"I'll explain later," I said. "Fate of the world at stake." I grabbed the milk from me, fifteen minutes earlier, through the tiny space-time portal.

"You must like milk a lot," said the globby aliens. "But that craving for lactic liquids will not make us take pity on you or let you go and spare your badly-designed planet."

"It should," I said. "What am I holding in my left hand?"

"Er. The milk," they said.

"And what am I holding in my right hand?"

They paused. Then one alien, so green and small and so globby and crusted that he might have been an enormous snot-bubble blown by an elephant with a terrible head-cold, said, ". . . the same milk from fifteen minutes earlier."

"Exactly," I said. "Now. Think about this one very carefully. What would happen if I touched these two things together?"

The globby aliens went a very pale green. The pirates, shiny-black-hair-men, and the piranhas looked at them, puzzled, seeking some kind of explanation, as did the wumpires.

"If two things that are the same thing touch," proclaimed the volcano god, "then the whole Universe shall end. Thus sayeth the great and unutterable Splod."

"How does a volcano know so much about transtemporal meta-science?" asked one of the pale green aliens.

"Being a geological formation gives you a lot of time to think," said Splod. "Also, I subscribe to a number of learned journals."

I coughed, in what I hoped was an ominous sort of way. "Well?" I asked.

"What he said," admitted the green globby aliens. "The bit about the Universe ending."

"So," I told them. "Unless you wish to spend the rest of your lives in a universe that no longer exists, you had better return things to the way they were. And then go away."

The aliens looked at each other. They grinned at each other.

One of them pressed the **grundledorfer**.

The wumpires, pirates, piranhas, volcano god, and the worshippers of the volcano god were gone.

"What if," suggested one of the green globby aliens hopefully, "we only redecorated the Southern Hemisphere?"

"Not a chance," I said. "Now, release us, or the milk touches itself! And then go away. Leave this planet forever."

The aliens looked at me, then they looked at each other, and then they sighed, with a noise like a hundred elephantine snot balloons all deflating at once.

"Right," they said.

It was at that moment that a voice louder than anything I have ever heard—and I had heard a volcano erupt at very close range—said,

"GALACTIC POLICE. DO NOT MOVE."

My hands shook, but the milk did not touch the milk, and the Universe did not end.

There were red and blue flashing lights and then, stepping off their space-bikes, were about half a dozen uniformed dinosaurs, holding unmistakably large and extremely serious weapons. They pointed their weapons at the green globby aliens.

"You are charged with breaking into people's planets and redecorating them," said a noble and imposing-looking Tyrannosaurus Rex. "And then with running away and doing it again somewhere else, over and over. You have committed crimes against the inhabitants of eighteen planets, and crimes against good taste."

"What we did to Rigel Four was **art**!" argued a globby alien.

"Art? There are people on Rigel Four," said an Ankylosaurus, "who have to look up, every night, at a moon with three huge plaster ducks flying across it."

Something very long with a head on the end of it came over to us. It was attached to a very large body, on the other side of the room. "Who are you?" it asked Professor Steg. "And why is your gorilla holding a transtemporally dislocated milk container?"

"I am not a gorilla," I said. "I am a human father."

"The human is holding the milk in order to make these evil redecorating snot-bubbles go away and stop menacing this planet and us," said Professor Steg.

The Diplodocus in a police cap opened its mouth and didn't say anything.

The Tyrannosaurus, who had handcuffed all of the green globby people together with something that looked a lot more like pink string-in-a-can than it looked like handcuffs, which was a good thing because they probably didn't have hands and they definitely didn't have wrists, stared at us and his eyes opened wide.

"Great day in the morning!" he exclaimed. "A biped. A Stegosaurus. A Floaty-Ball-Person-Carrier. . . ." And he stopped, as if unable to go on.

A Pteranodon flapped over to us, then landed at Professor Steg's feet. It looked up at him, and said, hesitantly, "Would you be . . . ? Could you be . . . ? The inventor of Professor Steg's **Pointy Zooming-into-Outer-Space-Machine**? Of Professor Steg's **Really Good Moves Around in Time Machine**? Would you be the author of *My Travels into the Extremely Far Future and What I Found There*? Professor Steg, wisest of all dinosaur-kind? **MADAM, IS IT TRULY YOU?**"

"It is," said the Professor. (**Madam?** I thought, embarrassed.) "And this is my assistant."

The Pteranodon extended a wing tip for me to shake, and without thinking, I moved the second milk from my right hand to my left . . .

Where the first milk was.

EVERYBODY GASPED.

Unfortunately, the milk

that had been in my right hand, which
was the same as the milk that was already
in my left hand, the same milk fifteen minutes
apart, *touched each other.*

I held my breath.

There was a fizzing noise, and a mewing as
if a hundred kittens were being agitated in an
enormous basket.

Professor Steg closed her eyes. "I can't
look," she said.

Three purple dwarfs with flowerpots on their
heads appeared from nowhere and began to do
a little dance.

"Did the Universe end?" said the
Tyrannosaurus, with his eyes tightly scrunched
closed.

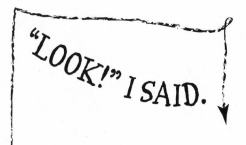

"LOOK!" I SAID.

We all watched the dwarfs dance. They weren't human and they weren't dinosaurs. They had purple skin and the flowerpots on their heads had lots of flowers growing out of them. They did a complicated sort of a dance, with lots of leg kicking and shouts of "*OY!*" and "*OLAY!*" and "*PERTUNG!*" And then, as strangely as they had come, they vanished.

"Ah," said Professor Steg. "It was always a possibility that this might happen. And fortunately, the Universe has not ended."

She pressed the button again, with her tail. A small hole in space and time opened up. I was standing on the other side with a baffled expression on my face.

"Catch!" I shouted, and threw the milk through the hole. As the portal closed, I saw me catch the milk using my stomach.

The green globby aliens having been rounded up and taken away, all the space-dinosaurs gathered around.

"I can't believe it," said the Diplodocus.

"Professor Steg. Just like in the comics. The dinosaur who taught us that in the far future, small mammals will eat their breakfast cereal with milk on it. Inventor of the button. She's here, in front of us, with her gorilla."

"Not a gorilla, but a human father," said Professor Steg, and all the other dinosaurs gasped and said things like "How wise she is!" and "What a brain!" and "How can you tell the difference between that creature and a gorilla? Is it the shoes?"

Professor Steg said, "This human father has been my companion on my strange journey into the future. Now, before I take my leave of him, and come with you, O Space Dinosaurs, we should sing to him one of the great old dinosaur songs."

They sang
me a song in six-
part harmony
called **"How Do
You Feel This
Morning When
You Know What
You Did Last
Night?"** Then
they sang me
a song called
**"Don't Go Down to the Tar Pits, Dear, Because
I'm Getting Stuck on You."** The Space Police
dinosaurs sang me a song about being Space
Police and saving people all over the Universe,
and driving very fast space-bikes. And then
they all sang a song called **"I've Got a Loverly
Bunch of Hard-hairy-wet-white-crunchers,"**
which was an ancient dinosaur song that had
apparently been written by Professor Steg's
Aunt Button.

There is nothing in the whole of creation as
beautiful as dinosaurs singing in harmony.

"Now," said Professor Steg. "I shall go off in my Floaty-Ball-Person-Carrier, with my newfound Dinosaur Space Police friends, and I shall explore the Universe, and then I shall return to my own time, and write a book about it."

"You actually write several books," said the Diplodocus. *"Professor Steg's Guide To Everything In The Whole Of The Future* was my favorite. It's very inspirational."

I said good-bye to all the dinosaurs. I thanked Professor Steg for saving my life.

"Not at all," she said. "We were both fortunate that you had the milk with you. It is not every container of milk that saves the world, after all."

"That was me that saved the world," I said. "Not the milk."

The space dinosaurs all had their pictures taken holding the milk and smiling at the camera.

"What are you going to do with the milk?" they asked me. "Are you going to put it in a museum?"

"No, I am not," I told them. "I am going to give it to my children for their breakfast cereal. And possibly I will pour some in my tea."

Professor Steg nipped back up the rope ladder and climbed into the gondola of her balloon. The last I saw of her—of any of them—the whole inside of the saucer was fading into light so bright I had to close my eyes and look away.

And then I was standing at the back door of our house, none the worse for wear. Fortunately, the dinosaurs had given me back the milk after they had their photos taken with it.

So I came in.

And here I am.

That was what my dad said.

I looked at my sister and my sister looked at me.

Then we both looked around the kitchen. At the calendar on the wall with the hot air balloons on it. At my dinosaur models and my sister's ponies, at my sister's vampire books, at the picture of a volcano I had painted when I was little, last year, and which is still up on the wall by the fridge. ⟶

We looked at those things, and we looked at my dad.

"You know, we don't believe any of this," said my sister.

"We don't," I told him. "Not any of it."

"Especially not how you saved the world from being remodeled. Or the pirates."

"Not. Any. Of. It," I said.

My father shrugged. "Suit yourselves," he said. "But it was all true. And I can prove it."

"How?"

"Yes. How?" asked my little sister.

"Well," said my father, putting it down on the kitchen table, **"here's the MILK."**

AND HE WENT BACK TO READING HIS PAPER.

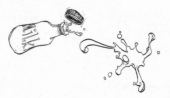